To Wyatt

Love the magic
of the moon

Karlene Kay Ray
IHN

Genevieve and the Moon

Story by Karlene Kay Ryan · Pictures by Meredith Johnson

My heartfelt gratitude to Ann Remen-Willis, Siri Weber Feeney, and Meredith Johnson. ~Karlene K. Ryan

Book designed by Siri Weber Feeney.
Typeset in Minya Nouvelle, designed by Ray Larabie of Typodermic Fonts.

Printed in the United States by Bookmasters, Inc.
30 Amberwood Parkway, Ashland, OH 44805
August 2013, Job #D12713

ISBN-13: 978-0-9888843-1-1

Karlene Kay Ryan
www.karlenekayryan.com

Dedicated to
Timothy,
Erin,
Keely,
Lauren,
Mark Jr.,
Seamus,
Cara,
and the
real Genevieve!

On the way to school one day, Genevieve said, "Mommy, I talked to the moon!"

The sun
didn't answer.
It just shone
warmly,
all alone
in the
blue sky.

Genevieve ran to her teacher.

Miss Janice! Miss Janice!
Where did the moon go?
It was there
last night.
I talked to it!
Do you
talk to the
moon, too?

Miss Janice smiled.

I like to say
'Hello Moon,
how are you?'
It shines back at me
like it's whispering
in a silent language.

Genevieve smiled, too.
She liked the quiet moon.

Later that day, Miss Janice said,
"Genevieve wants to know
where the moon goes in the daytime.
Who wants to help solve
the mystery?"

Timothy can be the moon and Maria, the sun. Genevieve, you can be the earth.
Me, too!
Classroom Costumes

"The sun shines on the earth . . .."
Miss Janice said.

Maria
switched on the light.

Is sunlight warm
or cool?

Warm!

Right!
The sun is really a star that's so close to the earth, we can see its brightness and feel its warmth.

The sun
turns off to make
night, right?

It seems like it would.
But, really, it's
because the earth
spins
as it turns around
the Sun . . ..

Genevieve spun slowly as she circled around Maria.

The sun shines *all* the time. When it's nighttime for us, it's daytime for the children on the other side of the earth.
But what about the **moon?**

Miss Janice smiled.

It shines in the sunlight!
So I can see the moon shining when it's night for me.

That's right. What about now?
It's day on this side but now I can't see the moon!

You can't see me 'cause
I'm spinning behind you . . .
Spinning . . . Spinning . . .
Spinning . . .
Spinning . . . Spinning . . .
Spinning . . . Spinning . . .

Timothy! STOP!
Good thing
the *real* moon
doesn't
get dizzy!

Everybody laughed and clapped.
Now they knew where the moon
goes in the daytime!

Miss Janice smiled quietly,
like the moon.

Soon, it was time to go home.

That evening, the sky changed
from blue to pink then gold and orange.

Genevieve watched the sun dip
until it disappeared.

"Sun's gone," said Daddy. "Bedtime."

"Say your prayers now and sweet dreams," Daddy said. "The Moon will shine on you while you sleep."

Tucked in bed, Genevieve
saw stars twinkling in the night sky.
It felt like they were singing to her.

She was asleep before she
heard their answer.

Late into the night,
something woke Genevieve.

A beam of silvery light
glowed gently through the window,
just like Daddy said.

"Hi Moon," she whispered.
"We did a play about you today.
When you visit the children on the
other side of the earth, will you
say hello from me?"

The moon smiled in its quiet way.

I see the Moon
The Moon sees me.
God bless the Moon
And God bless
Me.